THE CHRISTMAS TOY MACHINE

STORY AND PICTURES BY JANET WINTER

© THE MEDICI SOCIETY LTD · LONDON · 1996   *Printed in England*   ISBN 0 85503 183 2

On a bright December morning Father Christmas
heard a knock on his workshop door.

"Good morning, Father Christmas," said a cheerful little man. "I am Professor Plumb-Jamb; I have come to help you. I have just invented a completely new modern toy machine. It will make all your toys faster than you can imagine."

"But," said Father Christmas, "I'm not
sure that I want to make my toys any faster."

"Nonsense," said Professor Plumb-Jamb, "your workshop is hopelessly old-fashioned. Now with my machine…

...you just drop in the toy parts – buttons – wheels – ears and arms – anything you need, press a button...

...and in a twinkling out will come
finished toys all ready for delivery."

Because it had just been invented...

...the machine needed a few adjustments.

Some of the toys did not come out quite right.

Father Christmas and the elves
worked frantically to fix them.

What with one problem and another, Father Christmas was rather late getting started on Christmas Eve.

"Don't worry," said Professor Plumb-Jamb, "I have added my new rocket power booster to your sleigh. It will give you the fastest ride ever."

The reindeer were not too pleased when they found
the rocket booster had been put on backwards.

Luckily, as the sleigh raced past
the moon, the rocket fell off.

Father Christmas hurried through his delivery list.

The reindeer were very helpful but…

...it was nearly morning when
he visited the last house.

When Father Christmas got home, he found Professor Plumb-Jamb and the toy machine were gone. "Don't worry," said the elves. "He promised to come back next year—with an *improved*, even *better* toy machine."

"OH, NO!" said Father Christmas. "Next year I'm going to do everything the old-fashioned way."